Published in 2020 by Alligator Products Ltd.
Cupcake is an imprint of Alligator Products Ltd.
2nd Floor, 314 Regents Park Road, London N3 2JX

Written by Gaby Goldsack
Illustrated by Emma Leach

Copyright © 2020 Alligator Products Ltd.

All rights reserved.
No part of this publication may be reproduced or distributed in any form
or by any means without the permission of the copyright owner.

Printed in China.1665

Little Mouse Finds a Friend

cupcake

One winter, Foxglove Farm was covered in a soft blanket of snow. Little Mouse sat in the barn and shivered. He was cold and hungry. He knew there were tasty scraps and a warm fire in the farmhouse.

But he didn't **dare** go in there.

Entering the farmhouse was a **deadly** business.

First you had to get past the **huge** farm dog.

His **ferocious** bark and **snarling** teeth were enough to scare the bravest of mice.

Then there was the farmer's wife. It was said that she once cut off a mouse's tail with a carving knife.

But worst **of all was** . . .

... the **cat.**

She was **terrifying!!!**

She had dagger-like fangs and claws as sharp as needles.

Her **large** amber eyes saw everything.

And her small black ears missed nothing.

She could hissssssssssss like a snake.
And snarl like a tiger.

Little Mouse had heard that the cat could creep up on you in total silence. And then pounce with deadly speed.

The mere thought of the cat made Little Mouse quake with fear.

The days past and Little
Mouse became more and more
hungry. Each day he roamed the
farm in search of food
but there was little
to be found.

The horse guarded his oats.

The chickens chased him away from their grain.

The cows stamped their feet every time he tried to share their morning feed.

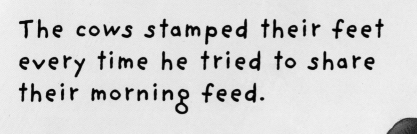

The pigs wouldn't even let him share the kitchen scraps.

By mid-winter Little Mouse was so hungry that he made a big decision. He was going to creep into the farmhouse and find something to eat.

That night, Little Mouse waited until the dog was asleep in his kennel and the farmer and his wife were snoring in their bed. Then he crept across to the farmhouse and peered in through the window. What he saw inside made him squeak with terror.

The cat was leaping up and down and spitting wildly.

Her hairs were standing
on end and her eyes glinted dangerously.
It was a terrifying sight.

Little Mouse was about to scamper away when the cat howled and flopped to the ground.

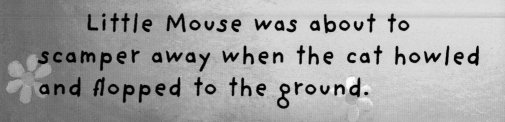

Miaow!

The sound made Little Mouse stop and take another look. It was only then that he noticed something. Something that gave him the courage to sneak in through the cat flap for a closer look.

The cat's right paw was stuck in a hole in the floorboards. As Little Mouse watched, the cat tried to tug her paw free but she only managed to hurt herself.

"Ouch!"

hissed the cat. Her amber eyes glinted with pain.

Little Mouse was very scared but he was also very kind. He didn't like to see anything in pain, so he crept forward to see if he could help.

The cat's ears twitched.

"Who goes there?" she hissed.

"Only me," squeaked Little Mouse bravely. "Can I help you?"

The cat swished her tail and sighed.

"My paw is trapped but I don't suppose a little fellow like you can help. I'll just have to wait until the farmer's wife comes down in the morning."

She began to lick her trapped paw so sadly that Little Mouse felt quite sorry for her.

"I **can** help," he declared bravely.

And before he could change his mind, Little Mouse dashed forward and began nibbling at the wood surrounding the cat's trapped paw.

Little Mouse tried to ignore the cat's glittering eyes as he gnawed away.

He tried not to think about her glistening fangs and sharp claws. He worked quickly and soon the cat's paw was free.

"Thank you,"

purred the cat.

She licked her sore paw
and arched her back with delight.

Her eyes glowed.
Little Mouse tried to flee
but the cat was too fast.
She pounced and trapped
Little Mouse's tail beneath
her paw.

"Hey, don't run away," she purred. "I'm not going to hurt you."
     Little Mouse gulped and looked up into her eyes. What he saw surprised him. Her eyes weren't scary at all. They were kind and playful.
Little Mouse smiled up at the cat.

"Yum!"

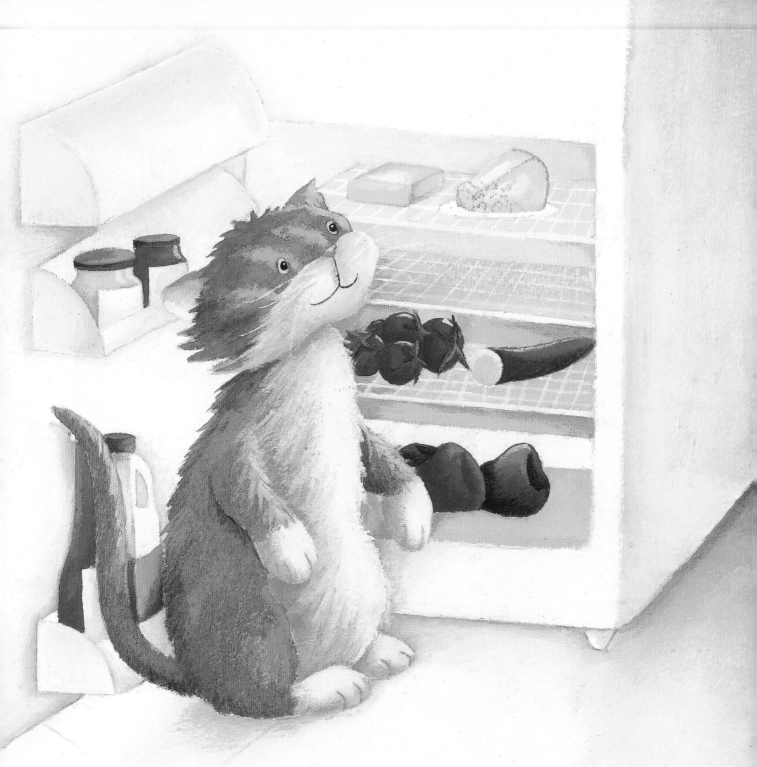

The cat smiled back, "Why don't you come and warm up by the fire?" she asked. "I can even find you some scraps of cheese if you like."

"Ooooo, yes please," squealed Little Mouse. "I am starving."

After Little Mouse had eaten so much that he groaned with pleasure, he sat beside the warm fire with the cat. By sunrise, Little Mouse and the cat were the very best of friends. Little Mouse had been wrong, the cat wasn't at all frightening. She was the friendliest cat any mouse could wish to meet.

Unfortunately, the farmer's wife didn't share this view on mice.

she **screamed**

and **screamed**

and **screamed!**

"Humans are frightened of mice," explained the cat. "That's why they make such a fuss."

"But what about the farmer's wife cutting off our tails with a carving knife?" asked Little Mouse.

"Oh, that's just a silly story," laughed the cat.

"But I think it's probably safer if you only come into the farmhouse when everyone else has gone to bed," the cat said, smiling.

From that day on, Little Mouse never went hungry.

Every day, the cat would leave little scraps of cheese inside his mouse hole in the barn.

And every night, when everyone else was asleep, Little Mouse would creep into the farmhouse and warm himself beside the fire with his **new best friend.**

The End.